Maurice Sendak

Seven Little Monsters

HarperCollins*Publishers*

Seven Little Monsters

Seven Monsters in a row, see the Seven Monsters go!

One goes up

Two goes down

Three comes creeping into town

Four eats only tulip trees

Five drinks all the tumbling seas

Six sleeps late but not in bed

Seven just screws off his head

Seven Monsters in a row, making trouble. There they go!